Light and Shadow

Foreword

It seems to me that no moment in life is one hundred percent totally wonderful. Nor is it, thankfully, one hundred percent totally awful. You might be in the middle of a good bit, when you get bad news. Or, you might be in the middle of a dreadful patch, when something hopeful happens. In other words, life is rarely either all sweetness and light or all gloom and doom. Instead, it's sort of light and shade at the same time, dappled in fact.

That's the idea behind this, my third, collection of short stories. The characters in the stories experience good bits and bad bits of life, light and shadow, often at the same time.

I offer the stories, as always, just because they were fun to do! I could say that writing short stories keeps me out of trouble. But then you might think these stories are trouble enough!

I hope you find something in them that you enjoy.

Tessa Woodward

(For recordings of some of these stories, please visit www.tessaswriting.co.uk and click on the 'Short Stories' tab.)

Light and Shadow

The House in Kamakura

Sometimes, before I go to sleep at night, I go back to that house in Japan.

I get off the black bike I had there, lean it against the bushes, and walk the woodland hiking trail up to the front gate. I step from stone to stone on the pathway to the side door, remembering the time I arrived to find a snake curled up asleep in the sunshine on the warm doorstep. I had to retrace my steps that day and, from a safe distance, stamp my feet until the vibrations caused the snake to wake up, yawn, and slip away.

The key went into the doorknob, as I recall. And the door swung outwards to reveal the *genkan*, the traditional entryway to a Japanese house. There, you take off your outdoor shoes and step up into the house, where your indoor slippers are waiting for you.

When you first come to Japan, it takes a while to figure out the procedure for entering a house. You take off one pair of shoes and turn them round so that they're facing out towards the door you've just come in, ready for your exit. And then you step up and into your slippers. You worry about if your feet might smell, about the state of your socks and whether they match what you're wearing. But after some years there, your actions become streamlined. You turn and turnabout in a practised fashion, all the while calling out '*Tadaima*' meaning, 'I'm back with you!' And the people in the house call '*Okaeri*!' meaning, 'You're welcome back with us!'

And, when it's time to leave the house again, you make your way to the step above the Genkan. You step out of your house slippers and turn them around so that they face back into the house. You step down into your outdoor shoes, which are of course facing the right way for exit. You call out '*Ittekimasu*!' which means, 'I'm going and coming back!' The people in the house call, '*Itterasshai*!' which means 'Go and come back!'

Light and Shadow

I went into that house in Japan for the first time one summer's night forty years ago. My friend and I were in Kamakura on a day trip from Tokyo. We were just wondering which evening train to catch back when we bumped into a colleague, Eddy, an American married to a Japanese woman. He needed company, he said. His wife had recently left him. His house felt empty. Would we come with him? Stay overnight and catch a morning train home? Mornings were better. He could manage mornings.

Now, Japan is hot and humid in summer, even at night. So, by the time we'd climbed the slow lanes up to his little wooden rented house, I was hot and sticky.

Eddy called '*Tadaima!*' out of habit when we reached the Genkan. But nobody answered.

He showed me the tiny bathroom. While he and my friend settled into the downstairs five mat room with a bottle of whiskey, I stripped off and dunked myself clean and fresh with water, dipped from the upright Japanese bath, water that cascaded down onto the tiled floor.

That night we stayed up late listening to the tale of Eddy's broken romance. Then, as we were tired, he showed us to the room upstairs, rolled out a futon for us, then left us alone to rest while he faced his demons alone downstairs.

I fell asleep for a while but then woke up. It was still dark. The huge sliding windows on two sides of the room were open, allowing a refreshing through current of air, while their metal screens protected us from the whine and bite of mosquitos. An orchestra of chirping cicadas throbbed away outside in the night. A nearby grove of bamboo rustled its leaves like silk in the breezes. I lay in the dark, cool at last, with my friend sleeping gently by my side. Listening to the texture of natural sounds, I was happy. So happy that I didn't need to sleep again for hours.

'Coffee?' asked Eddy in the morning.

Light and Shadow

'Please,' I said, watching as he moved, slow and melancholy, to the stove.

'At least you have a beautiful place to live,' I said, trying to be helpful.

'I don't think I can stay here,' he said. 'Too many memories. Too sad.'

'Where would you go?'

'Oh, I'd just rent another place nearer town. More going on. More distractions.'

'Well, I think you'd be crazy to give this place up,' I said. 'But if you ever do, please tell me. I'd move in like a shot!'

'It'd be a long commute for you?' Eddy looked at me thoughtfully.

'I wouldn't care a bit.'

And that's how we left it.

About a month after my friend went to follow a Master's course in London, I got a call from Eddy. He'd tried to stay on in the house. But he just couldn't. Was I still interested? I was.

Eddy left everything I needed in the house. Pots, pans, dishes. He said he'd pick it all up later when he could face it. I moved in with one rucksack.

Ah! I remember, I remember!

I remember learning how to toss the futon quilt over the upstairs railing to air it in the sunshine in summer. How to empty, refill and heat the water in the Japanese bath so I could sit up to my chin in

Light and Shadow

a scalding soak in winter. How to use a soft brush on the *tatami* mats so I didn't hurt the woven rice straw. How to use the *kotatsu*, the low table with the heater underneath and the cheerful red quilt on top that you wrap around to keep your legs snug.

I remember hiding from the groups of school children climbing the hill path past my house. For if they saw me in the garden, they would stop and point and chant '*Gaijin! Gaijin*!' meaning 'Outside person!', 'Foreigner!'

If, at quiet times, I climbed the path myself, I reached a stone statue of a sitting Buddha nestled in the wooded hills above my house. Resting on the sunny dome of the Buddha's warm head, butterflies would open and close their wings in bliss.

In the temple at the end of the hiking trail, I'd watch as a monk held a brush, wet with ink, above thick paper, making the first downstroke of a Japanese character.

On festival night, I'd hear children chatting away as, in bright kimonos, carefully holding candle lanterns, they made their way to the local shrine.

Ah! Those enormous lilies in the garden! Opening their perfume and sending it into the house.

I remember, I remember.

I remember when I left the house for the last time, I murmured, '*Ittekimasu!* Even though I knew I would never be going back again.

But I do go back sometimes. In my mind's eye. I walk the path to the side door. I slip my outdoor shoes off. I step up. My slippers are there ready for me, facing the right way. I call, *Tadaima!* and the house answers me, *Okaeri!*

(This story was first broadcast on BBC Radio Kent Upload on May 4th, 2022)

The Fears of a Frequently Frightened Flyer

You'd think, wouldn't you? That by now, up here, in the stratosphere, my hair would be whipping around my face. You'd think the wind would be howling in my ears, like a sonic banshee, or a transatlantic tinnitus. You'd think G forces would be pinning me back, hard, in my seat as I scream along,

>up here,

>>at 30,000 feet,

>>>at 550 miles per hour.

Oh God, I wish the pilot wouldn't remind us.

But instead, there is no breeze, no sound, no sense of speed. Instead, a cotton wool stillness, prior to free fall. The world has been edited out and all that is left is this tin can capsule.

Light is limited to the porthole. Movement is limited by the metal belt buckle and the pressure on my knees from the grey seat in front of me, tipped back. Sound is limited to a dull grey noise, less interesting than static. My fear is only limited by my willpower.

So, cocooned in a polyester blanket, a helpless pupa, a worm in its cast, I try to forget, to avoid, to deny the fact that I am screaming along

>up here,

>>at 30,000 feet,

>>>at 550 miles per hour.

Light and Shadow

Oh, I wish that little video wouldn't remind me.

OK. Get a grip. Try to tune in to the normality of hot liquid in cardboard cups, of smiling trolley ladies and tiny, tiny toilets. For surely, if I can sip tea, and smile, all must be well? Surely?

I try to settle to the glossy pages of the in-flight magazine, noting the prices of perfume I will never smell, of bracelet watches I will never wear. Or hear go tick. Tock.

Oh, don't think about anything that goes tick tock.

Now, we seem to be going smoothly. Encouraged, I make a tiny movement. Retrieve a paperback from the net. I bought it from a carousel of best sellers, down there, on the beloved, beloved, ground.

Steady on now.

Look at the picture on the cover. Stay in the now. At this very moment, all is well.

Venture a turn of the head, slowly to the left, and then slowly to the right, to see the other people. How calm they look! Playing solitaire on their laptops, listening to music on their ear phones, wearing eyeshades, dozing.

I tell myself to breathe in, then breathe out. It seems to be possible to breathe in and breathe out. Do it again. Perhaps I will get there after all?

I'm not going to even think of the word 'turbulence'. I talked myself into doing this. I talked myself up through take off.

Now, I'm talking myself along. Later, with luck, I'll be able to talk myself down. Chances are, statistically, that it will be possible. To land. Safely.

Chances are.

(This story was first broadcast on BBC Radio Kent Upload on January 14th, 2021)

Orbit

He's out there on Agate Beach every day, no matter what the weather's like. On this coast we can get days, even in August, when the sea fog rolls in fast, like a menace, like ink blobs dropped into water, blotting out the usual distinctions of sky, horizon, sea and sand. Blurring them all into one. I'll think, oh he won't be out today, not in this. But then, even as the cotton wool fog softly binds and mutes the crashing Pacific rollers, he'll emerge. Tall, rangy, walking fast, his Husky running ahead of him.

I've watched him under November rain while it thunders down, blinding wet, sluicing water across the beach in rivulets. I've seen him bent almost double in screaming storm winds, trying to make headway towards the North end of the bay.

Other days, at dawn, the full moon late to bed and still hanging, a bright shiny disc, high above the ocean, he's out there, striding, purposeful, across the hard wet sand, towards the lighthouse at the South jetty. His dog, the Husky, black and silver coated, metallic chain jingling, runs ahead, its wild, pale blue eyes, striking as a seer.

Who is this man? Why does he need to walk the length and breadth of this enormous bay? Twice a day? And in every weather? I lift my head from the telescope, turn away and go back inside from the deck into the house.

The beach is the reason we bought this house in the first place. And later, still a young man, I used to walk it every day myself too. That was after Jeannie left me. Whenever the feeling of hurt got too much, I'd get out of the house and cross the narrow beach road in front. In amongst the broom and salal bush hedges

Light and Shadow

on the other side, there's my 'rabbit hole'. That's what I call the opening to a narrow cliff path down to the beach. Hard to see it unless you know it's there. Getting down it was easy for me then, overgrown and steep though it was. First, the shallow red gulch with overhanging branches, then the slippery, brown mud slope, finally the sand dunes. All the while, the ocean booming louder and louder, the Lord's loudspeakers. Coming out on high sand dunes, with the full stretch of the beach below me, I'd feel like it was *my* beach. It surely was my sanity in those early days. I'd disappear, like Alice, down the rabbit hole, and find a different world at the end of it and different each time too. Some days fair with a high cobalt sky, other days a wind pushing a ragged storm front overhead, like an aluminum pan lid, slowly blocking out the sunlight from our world. But the weather didn't matter. The beach always soothed me. A little.

These days that old hurt has subsided, somewhat. I'm tormented instead by the pangs of old age. A tiresome litany of ailing body parts, the stages of my cross. So that pathway down to the beach is difficult for me now.

...

'Orbit! Come!'

The Husky was up in the dunes, standing stock still, tail up and barking.

'Orbit! Here!' I could hear the young man shouting.

But the dog stood its ground, staring at me from some distance with its uncanny pale eyes.

'You devil, making me come to you!' I heard the young man mutter, as he emerged, climbing amongst the sharp, stiff dune grasses, his feet slipping deep into the sand at every step.

Light and Shadow

When he'd climbed to the top of the dunes, he found me sprawled awkwardly in the mud at the foot of the slope. I raised myself painfully onto one elbow. 'Call your wolf dog off!' I said.

'Orbit! Heel!' The dog went eagerly to him, wagging and panting. 'Good boy!' The young man, stayed back tactfully, his dog sitting quietly now at his heel. 'Had a bit of a tumble?' he asked.

'Some fool has made ruts in this trail,' I grouched. 'It's impossible to get down here safely anymore.'

'Orbit! Down and stay!' The dog accepted the command with good grace and lay down at the side of the path watching me. The young man came over to offer help.

'Let's get you up.'

I grudgingly accepted a little support and sat up slowly. 'I think I've hurt my ankle.'

...

So that's how we met, me and young Jeff, the young beach walker, and his wolf dog. He helped me that day. Got me back up the path somehow. Went and got his truck where it was parked. Put the dog in the back in a metal dog cage thing. Took me to the emergency room, came in with me, stayed. Brought me home, settled me in. Wouldn't take any money for gas. Nothing. Then, this week, he's visited with me several times. Done my shopping. He stays too. Like today. Doesn't seem to be in a hurry. Got time, it seems.

'You've got him well-trained, Jeff,' I called out, eying Orbit lying sacked out in the sun, in his usual spot on my deck. Fast asleep.

Light and Shadow

Jeff laughed. 'I think it's the other way round!' he said, crossing from the back door, carrying out two mugs of strong black coffee for us.

'Why do you call him Orbit?'

The dog flicked an ear at the sound of its name.

'There you go,' said Jeff, handing me a mug. 'Because he used to run round and round in circles like a mad thing when he was a pup. He loves to run.'

'Good guard dog?'

'No! He looks tough but he's a real softie. Way too friendly. Plus, he doesn't usually bark much.'

I settled back in my wooden chair, winced when my back pain caught. My left ankle, strapped up in elastic bandages, was propped up in front of me on an old orange crate he'd found in the garage. The three of us, two men and one dog, out on the deck at my place, overlooking the ocean. Most company I've had since the paramedics came that time.

I sipped my coffee and started awkwardly. 'I've never really thanked you for all your time and trouble. If you hadn't come along and found me on the trail that day, why...'

'Oh, some other guy with a nosy mutt would have come along and done the same,' said Jeff.

'Well, anyway,' I said.

'You bet!' he said.

We shared a companionable silence.

Jeff took his mug of coffee and stood near the deck rail. 'Great view of the ocean you got here, Bud.'

'Best on the coast. That beach down there is mine, all mine. From here, anyway!'

Light and Shadow

Jeff walked to the corner of the deck, noticing the telescope for the first time. 'Like star gazing, eh?'

'That <u>was</u> the idea. See, when the dragon first left me, taking my only beloved son with her, may she burn in hell for all eternity, I tried every trick known to man to distract myself.' I put my coffee mug down on the deck beside me and remembered.

'Made driftwood mobiles, painted, joined the beach clean ups, took classes at the Pacific Science Centre, walked for hours. Then I got the idea that if I looked up at the stars, I would get some perspective.'

I stopped, closed my eyes, seeing only internal landscapes. I didn't finish.

When I opened my eyes again, Jeff was turned away from me, looking at the ocean. Just listening, I guess.

I sighed. 'Problem was, I didn't know what I was looking at. I didn't know what all of it was. What any of it was. I just saw hurt wherever I went, whatever I did and whatever I looked at.'

Nothing was said for a minute or two.

'Take my advice, Jeff,' I said, trying to make a joke out of it. 'Stay away from the uppity young ones. Those Delilahs. They're not worth the time nor the trouble. Nor the expense neither, for that matter!'

He didn't say anything.

Orbit whimpered in his sleep, his legs twitching. Chasing rabbits in his dreams I shouldn't wonder.

Light and Shadow

Jeff turned round from the rail and faced me. He considered me carefully. I couldn't guess what he was thinking. Not pity, I don't think. Probably wondering how many decades this fool old man had been nursing his hurt. Making a mental note not to do the same, most like.

'I find having a dog helps,' he said quietly.

Well. I stopped breathing for an instant. I started to form a couple of questions in my head, but they sounded clumsy to my mind's ear. I didn't know what to say.

The minutes passed. My chance went with it.

'Well, I guess I'd better go. Orbit needs a run,' he said.

'It's been dandy,' I heard myself say, as if I was ending something. Cursed old fool.

Jeff hesitated. 'Well, you have my number if you need anything.'

'Yeah,' I said. A familiar old pang deep inside returned, making it hard for me to breathe.

He whistled to the dog and turned to go.

I managed to get something out.

'Course, you know, Orbit's welcome to sleep on the deck here any time he likes.'

Jeff smiled. 'I guess he might like to do just that, Bud,' he said.

Light and Shadow

I heard them clump down the steps from the deck and then cross the road. The dog's chain jingled up the road a ways. Until they got to the 'rabbit hole,' I guess. Then I heard them no more, that day.

Light and Shadow

The Child That Never Was

The elderly woman, head bobbing slowly, swam breaststroke back to the shallow end of the public swimming pool. That made forty-two lengths. Her best ever. Pleased, she leaned back against the pool wall and rested a while. She watched the sunlight from the poolside windows dappling the warm turquoise water. To her left were the fast lanes, where adept swimmers were carving their way through the water creating frothy wakes, turning at each end like somersaulting dolphins. She, however, was in the slow lane. 'In more ways than one, these days,' she thought.

To her right was the general swimming area. No lane markers there. Just a large area for families to play in. Sunday lunchtime was usually quiet though. Just one young mother today, holding her baby close to her chest as she dipped and bobbed carefully in the lapping water. The young woman was singing quietly to her child. A made-up song. Something about splish, splash, sploosh. As she sang, she dipped just low enough each time to give the child the gentle feel of warm water on her feet and ankles. No further. Safe.

There was a time when the elderly woman could not have watched this. Any sight of a mother and baby in an affectionate moment together would cause a deep pang of loss and regret. Now, not wanting to make the young mother feel self-conscious, she turned her gaze back to her swimming lane. She lowered her goggles over her eyes. Another two lengths perhaps? She swam off and let her thoughts roam.

So ironic, to have tried so hard NOT to get pregnant in her teens and twenties. To have NOT wanted children so much that she had even saved up an abortion fund just in case that calamity should strike. So ironic to have believed back then that, if she did have a dalliance with someone without taking precautions, even just once, she would fall pregnant immediately. One time, one sperm and tra la that would do it! Ha!

Light and Shadow

So strange that, even in all those years of being ultra-careful, she still had imagined that, one day, she *would* have children. She'd often found herself having imaginary conversations in her head with an imaginary daughter, telling her this, teaching her that. When did those imaginary conversations with the imaginary child gradually fade away? She couldn't remember.

At the deep end of the pool, she reached up for a handhold on the wall and felt for a ledge for her toes. She rested a moment, remembering the years of remarks, often made to her by other women.

'You're not a real woman until you've had children,' one had said.

'Women who don't have kids are just plain selfish,' another had said.

'Try putting on a bit of weight, try placing this fertility symbol under your pillow, try crystals, try.....'

She remembered too those years of thinking up amusing or diverting responses to the ghastly question, 'Do you have children?' Or the even more bizarre follow-up question, 'What about grandchildren then?' Honestly, some people really had no idea.

She pushed off from the wall thinking of the years of 'trying' that had, for a while, changed making love with her man from something natural, spontaneous and joyful into a ritual dance of thermometers and charts, dates, duty, and monthly disappointments. When that was all over, she'd still thought that she might be an Aunty or a God Mother or something, even a babysitter for neighbours. But Fate had decreed that, for her, in the Children's Department of The Store of Life, the shelves would always be bare. Fortunately, there were other departments.

She rolled onto her back to try a lazy backstroke. There were too many people on the planet anyway, she thought. And they'd been happy together, her man and her. Truly happy, with time for each other, for friends, for travel, for hobbies. She turned again and, holding her breath, dived under the water to enjoy the patches of

Light and Shadow

light playing on the bottom of the pool. She was amused at the sight of the swimmers in the next lane, wriggling their legs like tadpoles.

She felt suddenly grateful for it all. For health, for the swim, for her man, for her life. She may not have had child luck, but she had had all kinds of other luck. It's a question, she decided, of wanting what you have, rather than the other way around.

Back at the shallow end, she ducked under the lane marker, stood up, and took off her goggles.

'Is she getting used to it?' she asked the young mother.

'I think so. As long as she has this!' The young woman touched the pink plastic dummy in the baby's mouth.

'Good idea to start young,' said the elderly woman, smiling at the baby. Then, 'Do you like the water, little one?'

The baby considered her with serious eyes for a moment then hid her face shyly in her mother's neck.

'When you think about it, they spend their first nine months of life swimming really, don't they?'

'Yes, and this one was kicking like a frog for most of that time!' said the young woman. 'Ouch!'

They both laughed.

'Well, you're doing beautifully now,' said the elderly woman, as she waded past.

The young woman's expression softened. 'Thanks!' and added, 'Nice to meet you.'

'You too,' said the elderly woman, pulling herself slowly up the metal ladder at the side of the pool. She felt pleasure at the encounter. Still, best not to tarry, just in case.

'How many lengths did you do today?' asked the pool attendant. She was often on at Sunday lunchtimes.

Light and Shadow

'Forty-four, I think. Unless I lost count somewhere!'

'Well done! More than I usually do!'

(This story was first published on the Mayah's Legacy website, here:

https://www.mayah.org.uk/post/thechildthatneverwas-shortstorybytessawoodward)

Light and Shadow

Just the Ticket

The traffic warden strolled along the tree-lined street, pausing every now and then to check the number plates of the parked cars. On such a hot day, it was pleasant there under the trees, so she took her time. Most of the cars, she noted with satisfaction, had been manoeuvred into the parking spaces with care, well within the white lines of the 'Four hours only' bays. Nice to see that people had too, for the most part, sensibly hidden away any tempting items. No laptops or phones on view.

She wandered along the line of cars and then saw it. Still there. That swanky silver estate car from several days ago. She checked the registration number to make certain. Yep. Same car. The windscreen and bonnet were now covered in blossoms and pollen after standing under the summer trees for days. The 'Penalty Charge Notice' she'd taped to the windscreen on Wednesday was still there. She wiped the plastic envelope until the words 'DO NOT REMOVE' were again clearly visible. Walking around the car, she noted that there was no body damage, as yet. Tyres still alright too. But if the owner left it there much longer, nice car like this, it might get vandalised. Well, the next step would be a letter sent to the registered owner. Then, if there was still no response, it'd have to be towed. She peered inside and saw a pair of women's black leather shoes on the passenger seat. She could make out a number 38, on the insole of one. Had the owner had an accident? Ended up in A and E? She wandered off, musing.

The owner of the size 38 shoes, Eva, had sat in the estate car for over an hour the morning she'd parked it, realising gradually that she couldn't go home anymore. Then a stray image, a memory, of deep blue stained-glass windows in the cathedral in Chartres had come to her. And, on a whim, she'd changed into her trainers, checked she had her passport, locked the car and was gone.

Light and Shadow

Later that day, on the Train à Grande Vitesse, rattling towards the city of Chartres in hot sunshine, she'd dozed, seeing nothing, hearing nothing, exhausted. The train sped across the Beauce plain. On the horizon, Chartres cathedral with its two towers rose out of the flat land, a medieval miracle, an ark sailing on a dry sea of wheat.

Arriving in Chartres, muzzy headed from the heat and her doze, she wandered the familiar streets, stopping to pick up a toothbrush and other essentials. Then, the half mile to the cathedral. Pushing open the stiff door, she slipped in. She passed the holy water basin, and the flickering rows of visitors' candles, found a seat in the cool and dark and sat down. As her eyes adjusted, she lifted her head and gazed up at the stained glass in the cathedral windows. Mosaics of intense translucent colour, each panel surrounded by curves and bars of lead, they told ancient stories unfamiliar to Eva.

After an hour, refreshed from the drench of colours, she went looking for the cathedral labyrinth. She knew from past visits that it was nothing like the green mazes found in the grounds of English castles; those verdant, physical puzzles designed to block the sight of promising paths with their high hedges. This labyrinth was two-dimensional, circular, some 12 metres in diameter, and laid out in stones of different colours on the floor of the cathedral. When the floor was cleared of ranks of chairs, as it was today, the circle could be used as a walking meditation. Everyone who stepped into the stone floor pattern entered at the same point, encountered easy and difficult stretches, journeyed into the centre, found a way out. Eva wondered how many thousands of people had walked on it over the centuries, wearing the stones of its concentric circles as smooth as seashore pebbles, understanding the labyrinth as a metaphor for life. On stepping in and slowly walking forwards now, she came to a choice. Walk ahead on a gentle curve or make a tight U-turn to the right.

Light and Shadow

She chose the gentler curve but a minute later arrived at a cul de sac marked in darker stone. She hesitated. She was stilled, suddenly tired of obstacles and dead ends, suddenly weary and uneasy. She stepped out of the labyrinth, walked back to the main door and escaped into the sunshine outside where she stood for a minute, blinking.

Many of the people staying at her hotel were Brits breaking their journey down to the Dordogne or to Provence. The place was friendly, clean and cheap, especially if you booked over the internet, as Eva had done, on the train.

'On your way down or on your way back up?' asked the woman who came across the terrace to sit at the table next to Eva.

'Neither. I'm staying here for a couple of days,' said Eva. 'I saw the cathedral windows last time I came and just fancied seeing them again. Spur of the moment kind of thing.'

As they were ordering dinner at the same time, the waitress assumed the two women were friends and pushed their tables together. Finding the idea agreeable, they ate and talked together companionably. It wasn't long before Eva's story came out.

'Oh my God!' said Ann. 'So, what sort of a mess have you left behind?'

'A bloody awful one,' said Eva. 'I have no idea what I'm going to do. When we were getting on well, at the start, he sold his house and moved all his stuff into my house. But pretty soon I knew it was a mistake. First of all, it turned out that he was allergic to dogs. So, I had to give my poor old dog away to a friend. Then he was unpleasant to my lodgers so eventually they moved out.

Light and Shadow

Their rent had been an important part of my income. Then, the more we argued, the more I didn't want to have anything to do with him. I started sleeping in the guest bedroom. He took over the main bedroom. He's also taken over my office, where my computer is. I run my business from home, you see. At least I used to! It's just hopeless now. I asked him to move out but he refused. I've asked him again and again but he won't go. So now I'm stuck. I'm scared to go back to my own house cos he gets nasty, especially when he drinks, which is every night. I can't run my business from home. There's no money coming in from that or from the lodgers. I just don't know. I just….' She stopped and blinked.

'So, you ran away to look at some blue glass windows.'

'Yeah. It's what I'm good at, running away.'

There was a pause.

'Does this bloke ever leave the house or go away at all?'

'Not much. Mostly he watches sport on the telly, and films, and late-night porn.' Then Eva remembered. 'Oh yeah. He _is_ going to the wedding of one of his sons soon. Up in the Hebrides. It was planned months ago. We were going to go together. I even bought a new dress and sorted out the plane tickets for us both.' She sighed.

'How long's he away for?'

'About four or five days.'

'Hmmm, five days is plenty long enough.'

Eva looked at her companion's face, puzzled. 'Long enough for what?'

Ann smiled.

Light and Shadow

Back on the tree-lined street in England, at ten o'clock one evening, when the streets were quiet, a tow truck turned up. A man in orange overalls clambered down from the cab. He took a look at the dusty grey estate car.

'Tyres look all right,' he said to himself. 'Shouldn't be a problem.'

A woman was walking up the street. He didn't take much notice of her until she stopped near his truck, smiled at him and said, 'Oooh, that's lucky! I got here just in time!' She pressed the fob on her car key and the lights on the car flashed on and off once in response.

'You can't just get in and drive off, you know, Miss,' the man said, moving to stop Eva from opening the driver's door. 'This car has been parked in a four hour only zone for a very long time. It's been classified as abandoned.'

She dodged him and walked round to the passenger side.

'It's okay,' she said. 'I don't want to drive it. I've just come to pick up some shoes.' She opened the passenger door, reached in and grabbed a pair of black leather shoes from the front seat. Straightening up, she waved them at him. 'See! I just came for these.'

The tow truck man watched her warily. People sometimes got tricky at this point. He knew from experience.

'You've had parking tickets and two 'Penalty Charge Notices' too, he said.

Eva grinned at him. 'Yes, I can see that. They're still there on the windscreen.'

'And a formal notification sent to the registered owner of the vehicle.'

'Yes,' said Eva, laughing. 'It just arrived at my house. I read it.'

The man paused. This one was obviously a bit of a fruit cake.

'So, as the registered owner of the vehicle,' he went on, 'you now have to pay a fine before arranging to collect the vehicle from where it will be impounded.'

'Where's that?'

'A tow lot on the edge of town. You can get a map off the internet.'

'And what happens if nobody pays the fine or collects the car?'

'Well, then, after a certain time and various legal procedures, it will be sold at auction.'

'Ah! Who gets the proceeds?'

'The council.'

'I see.'

'It's to recover the cost of towing and the storage and all.'

'Sounds very reasonable,' she said.

Tow truck man looked at her. She seemed alright. 'Can't you afford the fine then, love?' He sounded like he was beginning to care.

'Oh, it's not my car,' said Eva. 'It belongs to my ex. I took it after he nicked mine and smashed it up. He took over my house too. And threatened me. Anyway, now he's gone away for a bit so I've changed the locks on him. The police know about him too so he can't come anywhere near the house.'

'Ah! Bit of a domestic, is it?' The man grimaced. 'And where does his lordship think HIS car, this car, is now?'

'He has no idea. I haven't seen him since I took it. He's in Scotland at the moment.'

'Are you going to tell him where it is when he gets back?'

Light and Shadow

'I hadn't planned to. This'll teach the bastard.'

The tow truck man chuckled. He looked at the young woman. Poor little thing, living with a bully.

'We usually get junky old cars to tow away,' he said. 'Ones that've been driven into the ground and then abandoned. Old clunkers. But non-derelicts, like this one, tax okay, tyres okay, perfectly drivable, there's nearly always a story behind these.'

'Do you want the keys?' Eva asked.

'Well, if you don't want 'em. Might make things a bit easier.'

Eva tossed the keys over. She sat down on the low brick wall separating the pavement from somebody's front garden. 'Mind if I watch?' she said, getting comfortable.

'Be my guest!' said the tow truck man, leaning into the car to check if the handbrake was on. He straightened up and looked at her. "Where d'you meet him then? No, wait. Let me guess. On the internet! Am I right? Or am I right?'

Eva sighed. 'You're right. But, you see, he looked so great on his profile.'

The Sturdy Boy

We'd not long moved into the road. Ken's early retirement package had helped us to get a place we both liked the minute we saw it. Detached, nice bit of garden front and back. Spare room just in case our niece came to stay. Room for the caravan. We'd settled in well and were beginning to get to know the area. Next door moved in after us. A couple with a young lad. Been in about a month or so, I should think. We'd noticed the boy making friends with our dog, Moxie, over the gate on his way to school. Still, it was a surprise when, one Saturday, he knocked on the front door. There he was, on the step, sturdy legs planted wide, toes sticking out the front of his old plimsolls.

'Can I take your dog for a walk?' he asked.

'What?'

'I'll be careful with her. Can I?'

'You're the boy who comes past mornings?'

'Yes. I live there.' He pointed to next door. 'I'm Alan.'

Moxie was hurling herself at him in delight.

'She likes me. I think she'll come with me alright.'

I hesitated. But he looked so sure somehow, all sandy hair and freckles.

'Where would you take her?'

'Just round the streets 'til she gets used to going with me?'

'Well, I can't see the harm,' I said. 'You'll keep her on the lead now, won't you?'

So that's how it started. He'd turn up after school or on weekends. Once he was sure the dog would stay with him, he'd take Moxie up the moor for long rambles.

Light and Shadow

Afterwards, in the kitchen, he'd tell Ken and me about the hares, pheasants and buzzards he'd seen. And hungry? He could get a packet of biscuits down him faster than I could say 'Hot chocolate or Pepsi?'

He was an unusual lad for these days. No smart phone. No hoody. And when Ken slipped him a bit of cash to thank him for walking the dog, what did he spend it on? Treats for Moxie and a brush so that he could sit in the garden and groom her for hours on end. His parents didn't seem to mind. Never came looking for him or anything.

He didn't seem to have many friends. Said the boys in his class couldn't tell an Oak tree from an Ash. Turns out, he'd come from a village near Gloucester, not that far from where I was brought up. An only child too, like me. But you could tell he'd been happy there with his Mum and his real Dad. Loved going to his Grandparents too, on a smallholding nearby. He said his Dad used to take him fly fishing on the River Wye. Had shown him how to make lures, to cast, and reel the line in slowly. There was something odd about it all but we didn't pry. We knew if he wanted to tell us, he would. And he did.

'My Dad topped himself,' he said one day. 'The boys at school said it was my Mum's fault. That she'd been having it off with someone. I got into scraps with another boy at school about it. The teacher asked me why I was fighting but I wouldn't tell him. Well, I wasn't going to repeat what the other boy had said about Mum, was I? So, the teacher thought I'd started it. Said I had to control my temper. I got him good though, that other boy, later.'

Bit by bit the full story came out. It was true, it turned out, that Alan's Mum had taken up with somebody, a man called Ray who moved in shortly after Alan's real Dad died. Acted quite nice to the boy at first. Promised him a dog of his own. That sort of thing.

'He's never said another word about me getting a puppy though. Not since we got here. And he's always picking on me.

Light and Shadow

Mum says I've got to call him "Dad". But I don't like him. Noisy dirty boots all over the house. Loses his temper. Worse than I do. I just call him Ray. He doesn't care what I call him anyway.'

When Alan started staying on with us 'til dinner time, I worried that his Mum might wonder where he was. Ken popped next door to explain that we weren't kidnapping the boy. They didn't seem that bothered where he was, to be honest. Never got in until late anyway.

One day, mid-morning, as we came in from shopping, we spotted Alan sitting on the front steps.

'That's funny,' I said. 'It's a school day.'

'Coming in for a cuppa and a biscuit, lad?' Ken said casually.

The boy followed us in without a word and sat down. Moxie jumped straight into his lap and licked his face. He didn't even smile. Just sat and stroked her. We put the shopping away. Then I made a cup of tea and put an open packet of biscuits in front of Alan. He didn't take one.

'What's up lad?' said Ken sitting opposite him at the kitchen table.

'Mum's thrown me out.' He looked close to tears.

'Why's that then?' said Ken.

'Last night, Ray was picking on me again. He told me to eff off to my room. I told him to eff off straight back and ran upstairs. I could hear them rowing about it all night. When I came down this morning, Mum said I was making trouble between them and it'd be best if I didn't live there anymore.'

'What are you going to do, kid?' I said.

Alan looked down at the kitchen table.

'Tell you what,' I said. 'Do us a favour and give Moxie a little brush in the back yard?'

Light and Shadow

Alan nodded. He lifted Moxie carefully onto the floor and went to find her brush.

'Take your time. Supper will be a little while yet,' I said.

Once the lad had gone outside, Ken and I talked it over. 'This new man, Ray, is obviously more important to his Mum than her own son,' I said.

'Yeah, I don't think she cares two hoots about the boy,' Ken agreed. 'Never seems to care how long he stays with us evenings. I wonder if his grandparents in Gloucester would have him. He seems fond of them anyway.'

I found Alan's mother at home that night. 'It's only me from next door,' I said.

'I know who you are,' she said, narrow faced.

'If it's convenient,' I said. 'We wondered if Alan could stay with us a while. He's so good with the dog, you see. And it might keep him out from under your feet?'

She said nothing.

'We thought he might like to come caravanning with us in the school holidays too, if you didn't mind?'

'The little tyke lives round your place all the time anyway,' said Alan's Mum, all waspy like. 'But you'll have to watch him. He nicks stuff.'

'Well, thank you for the warning,' I said. 'If I could just trouble you then for some of his school clothes for the morning?'

She went upstairs, leaving me on the step. I could just see an open door into a sitting room. The corner of a sofa. A TV was on, blaring.

'Where're you going in the caravan then?' she said, handing over some school shirts and trousers.

Light and Shadow

'We were thinking we could go Gloucester way,' I said carefully. 'Alan says he has a bit of family there?'

She gave me a long look. She'd got my drift.

'Alright,' she said. 'Might be for the best,' and closed the door.

When I got back to ours, Ken was in the kitchen. No sign of Alan. I put the kid's clothes on the back of a chair.

'Downright unnatural,' I said. 'All Mrs Next Door said was to watch Alan cos he steals things!'

'He's just told me that himself,' said Ken.

'Well, goodness, what did he steal?'

'Money out his stepdad's wallet. I asked him if he knew that was a wrong thing to do. He said he did but that Ray had stolen his Mum from his Dad so he didn't see why he shouldn't steal from Ray.'

'Sort of a logic to it, I suppose. Still. It's not right. Where's Moxie?'

'With Alan,' said Ken. 'In the spare bedroom.'

'Dog's not really allowed upstairs,' I said to Ken.

'I know but the kid seems more settled somehow, with the dog,' Ken said. 'Nearly the end of the school term anyway. They finish on Friday, he says. Don't suppose it'll do any harm for him to have Moxie up there for a night or two?'

'Don't suppose it will,' I said, going to the cutlery drawer. 'Well, I'd better lay up for breakfast in the morning. Early start for us!'

(A version of this story was first broadcast on BBC Radio Kent Upload on October 20 and 21, 2021)

Light and Shadow

Past Master

How long does it take to fall in love with a stranger? A talented, intelligent, knowledgeable and very pretty stranger? So thought the tall man standing at the back of the group on the 4.00 pm tour. About ten seconds max, he reckoned.

While she was talking about the first painting, he noticed her dark brown hair, pale complexion and lively, warm, brown eyes. He guessed Italian influences. He took in her slim waist in the modest dress, sleeves to elbows, hem to mid-calf, skirt swaying as she moved. And how she moved!

By the second painting, her gestures were becoming familiar. She would lift an arm, gracefully pointing things out on the canvas. She would rise up on her tip toes, balancing in soft black leather pumps, when referring to something at the top of a picture. He guessed, from her ease as she did this, that there was dancing in her past or present.

By the time he had watched her at the third painting, he had noted her independent mind and witty take on the differing attitudes to women in art over the centuries. He'd have to be careful what he said, then. He knew himself to be a male dinosaur. He'd been told.

His first wife used to tell him that he had the sense of humour of a character in an old time British 'Carry on' film. His second wife that he had the political correctness of Jeremy Clarkson from the TV programme 'Top Gear' and his third. Well, best not to think about his third wife. That restraining order she'd got the police to put on him was a real surprise. Harsh. He sighed. He just didn't get women sometimes. They seem to like you one minute and then bingo, the next minute they turn all nasty.

His thoughts came back to the tour guide. He watched her as she moved, as she spoke, as she looked about her. When listening to a question, she would look at the questioner with full attention.

It made him want to ask her something, just to get the benefit of that steady look. But he was careful. He didn't want to draw attention to himself. Yet.

She glanced at her wristwatch only once, at the end of the tour. Then, accepting everyone's thanks, she turned and, with her quick, quiet step, was off.

He assumed she would go back to some office behind the scenes. He saw her as a full-time member of staff. Perhaps she was the one who wrote the notes for the gallery web site.

He stepped outside the building for a little air and stood still for a moment, trying to get his bearings. A tall, well-built man, it was hard to tell his age. Mid-sixties? He was dressed on the formal side of casual, in a navy blazer, straight cut trousers, and brown leather loafers. A Rolex watch and rolled up Burberry umbrella betrayed his love of luxury brands. As he looked about him, he caught sight of the neat brunette, his gallery guide, coming out of a side door. She hesitated on the threshold, engrossed in the little lighted screen of her mobile phone. Then, smiling to herself, she stepped into the street. She walked away across the square, slim and dark, the black dress swaying with a lilt. And he was suddenly desperate to know her.

Without thinking, he made a move to follow her. But after a few steps he caught himself and made himself stand still. He watched her as she crossed the square headed for the stone steps at the far side. Running lightly down them, she bobbed out of view. She was gone. His heartbeats came full and fast.

Good God! he swore to himself, there are more subtle ways of following a woman than thundering up behind her at a tube station. Anyway, he'd spotted her name on her identity badge. He turned back towards the main door of the gallery.

As he approached the information desk, he noted that the woman on duty was rather plain. Perfect.

'Hello! I wonder if you can help me?' he said, displaying his most charming smile. 'I'm interested in the Fine Arts. I'd like to come

Light and Shadow

to the gallery regularly to take advantage of the free talks and tours. In fact, I've just been on a fantastic hour's tour with Megan Williams.' He searched the woman's face for recognition of her colleague's name. 'She is so knowledgeable, so good at making things clear!'

'Oh yes, she is!' the woman agreed. 'I've taken her tours too!'

They smiled at each other. 'Good,' he thought. 'This is working nicely.'

'I'd like to attend more of her talks, maybe even a day long workshop or a course, if she does them?'

'Yes, Megan does talks twice a week. And then she works with a travel company for her courses abroad.'

'Interesting! Which company is it?'

He pumped her for as much information as he dared. 'Thank you so much! You've been so helpful!' He gave her what he hoped was a rakishly warm twinkle and strolled out of the gallery to a nearby café. Once installed there with a creamy coffee, he set to work on his laptop.

The basics were easy. Her name led to a photo and details on a professional networking website. From that, he learned where she went to university, which countries she'd lived in…. yes, he was right, Italy! …. what her specialities were. There we are, dance and drama! He congratulated himself on his instincts. He sat back, sipping his coffee. She hadn't looked like a woman trammelled by kids somehow. He wondered which dating sites she would prefer.

He knew most of them. Not a Telegraph reader he didn't think, judging from her remarks on the tour. He narrowed it down to sites connected to left wing and middle-of-the-road, national newspapers. A subscriber to these himself, since he would describe himself as 'educated, romantic and discerning', he scrolled through the profiles, filtering swiftly by age, area and interests. One hour and twenty minutes later and bingo. He was

Light and Shadow

pretty sure from the photo, the nickname she had chosen for herself, and the mini profile, that it was her.

He lowered the lid of his laptop a little, pleased with the afternoon's events. Giving the waitress a broad smile, he ordered another coffee. Best to stay away from the gallery for a while before contacting her via the dating site. Just in case she recognised him from his photo, even though it had been taken a while ago.

It took a month of carefully casual and good-humoured emailing to get a first meeting with 'Ms Florentine'. She'd obviously read the 'Guide to safe internet dating', as she proposed a mid-morning coffee in a very public place for their first date. When he got to the appointed place, he pretended to look around at all the women in the cafe to see which one could possibly be his date. He noted that she had already ordered her own coffee, to establish her independence. And was switching on her mobile phone, for security purposes most likely. He approached her table and waited for her to look up. She did so and looked surprised. Maybe he did look just that little bit older than his profile photo. That was probably it.

'You are perhaps 'Ms Florentine'?' he asked.

'Goodness!' she said. 'Are you William of Kent?'

He smiled and, after a pause, she indicated the empty seat opposite her. He sat down. She looked at him uncertainly.

'Would you like another espresso?' he asked her politely. 'Just while I have one?'

Appreciating this indication of a possible hasty exit on her part, she agreed. 'That would be nice!' she said with good grace. He turned around. The staff looked busy but he eventually managed to catch a waiter's eye.

'Another espresso for *La Signorina* and a cappuccino for me please.'

Light and Shadow

'I hope I haven't kept you waiting long?' he said courteously and continued, 'Bit of a delay on the tube from St Pancras where I came in.' He chuckled boyishly. Always good to provide a few openings for questions, he knew. Then he could be the first one to reveal a bit of personal information. Women felt more comfortable and secure once a man had done that.

But unexpectedly she didn't follow up. There was no, 'Oh, so you came in from out of town then?' or 'You speak a bit of Italian, then?' She only said, 'No, I've just got here.'

He caught her regarding him and then looking away. Perhaps a bit of prattling would help.

'Fantastic weather up here, isn't it? Where I live, in Kent, there's been this dreadful North wind blowing for months. It feels like it's coming straight from the Arctic! Slicing its way through the tender plants. I've been trying to get an Italian garden going at home, you see. Hopeless!'

After their coffee date, he'd gone for a stroll by the river. Puzzled, he considered what had happened. None of his usual ploys had worked. She'd never really settled, had stayed wary to the end. Nothing like the relaxed, confident person he'd seen at the gallery on the tour. He'd been careful not to ask her any personal questions. But she'd revealed not a single detail about herself. He'd given her plenty of opportunities to ask him about himself. She'd not taken them either. Instead, she'd kept the conversation relentlessly to the here and now, commenting only on the window boxes of the café and the strength of the bloody coffee, for God's sake! She'd received the usual, obligatory phone call twenty minutes in. Obviously, she'd asked a friend to call her at a certain time. He was used to that.

'That was work, I'm afraid,' she'd said, snapping her phone shut. 'Something's come up. Sorry, I have to go. Thanks for the coffee.'

He'd risen to his feet a little stiffly. Knees not what they were.

'My pleasure entirely,' he'd said, knowing that it was probably the absolute truth.

And she'd gone. He felt a bit sore about it. But, also, not a little determined. After all, he had a lot of information about her. And he had always enjoyed the chase more than anything. Well, almost anything.

He sent her a brief, light email next day. Just saying how he'd enjoyed her company and hoping the work problem hadn't turned out to be too tricky. He mentioned in passing that he would be away on business for a few days. Women like to hear from you after a date. But they don't like to be chased too hard, he knew that.

Over the next few days, he prowled around on Facebook and Twitter. She was very active on social media. Normal for a woman of her age, which he put at mid to late twenties. No sign of a steady boyfriend though.

He got into the habit of dropping Megan an email via the dating site every few days.

Just something cheery with, say, a photo of a plant from his 'Italian garden'. Never asking for a date. Occasionally he would get a cagey line back. But she gave nothing away, ever, so it was hard to get a hook or a line. He reconsidered his strategy. If he could get her to spend a little more time with him, he felt sure that she'd warm to him.

In his next email, he mentioned casually that he'd started to get interested in art again after many years. How wonderful the internet sites were for this sort of thing. And how brilliant were the free talks at so many of the provincial and metropolitan galleries up and down the country. He was taking in quite a few of them on his travels. Had she ever tried them? She did not reply. Worse yet, next time he tried to contact her via the site, he found that she'd blocked him! Stung, he waited a couple of days and then telephoned the 'Art Tours' company to book a place on her

Light and Shadow

next five-day tour around the galleries of Florence. He paid by credit card and was feeling smug about the surprise she was going to get when he turned up there. But a few days later, he received a letter by snail mail to say that the company telesales staff had made an unfortunate error. The tour was in fact fully booked. His card had been credited with the full amount he had paid. They hoped he would accept their apologies, 'for any convenience casued'. Can't even write bloody English, he thought.

On the ground floor of the art gallery, a group of people gathered near the sign that said,

'FOR 4.00 pm TOUR

PLEASE WAIT HERE'

The first to arrive was our tall, well-dressed man. Still bristling from his message from the travel company, his face flushed, he looked nettled. Others came in ones and twos, to wait nearby.

At 4.00 pm, the tour guide, Megan Williams, arrived. She stepped neatly into the waiting area and looked around.

'Anybody need the lift?' she asked.

Nobody said anything.

'Then we'll take the stairs. Please follow me!' She darted off. The group followed, the man with the flushed face bringing up the rear. They gathered round one painting and, after a very brief discussion, moved on.

As they moved towards the second painting, he noticed the tour guide taking out her mobile phone and making a quick call.

The tour was excellent the group agreed later. The guide had made witty remarks about the social mores and contexts of the paintings she'd chosen to introduce to them. She'd started with a French painting showing a man, hidden in some bushes, peering at a woman on a swing, waiting for her dress to blow up.

Light and Shadow

She'd described him as a 'Peeping Tom' and had said, to titters of agreement from her audience, that much art was like this really, just masculine wishful thinking.

They had then romped past a number of paintings all seemingly on the topic of women and refusals; women refusing glasses of wine, women refusing money, and women refusing the advances of men. The final painting was called *'Noli me Tangere'*. When someone asked what that meant, translated into English, the tour guide looked steadily around the group and explained. *'Noli me Tangere'*, literally, means 'Don't touch me!' Here, in this painting, it is, as you see, a request from Christ to Mary Magdalena. But over the years, the phrase has entered the artistic language and imagination. It's been used in all sorts of ways….in hunting pictures showing hinds being chased, for example. And it's come to represent the plea from the elusive one to the hunter, or perhaps we would say these days, the stalker. Thankfully,' she continued. 'Things have changed over the last few years. Now, when a woman says, "No!" most sane people understand that she means….?'

She indicated with an open-handed gesture that the group should finish her sentence.

'No!' they murmured, amused. Megan cupped one hand behind her ear. 'Couldn't hear you!' she said playfully.

'NO!' they said louder and then laughed as other people in the gallery turned to see what was going on.

Megan glanced quickly at her wristwatch and thanked them for coming on the tour. She hoped that they had learned something that would stick. As members of the group stayed behind a moment to thank her personally, the older man, looking sour, sauntered to the exit door. He did not notice the security guard right behind him until he got to the threshold of the building.

The security guard moved closer. 'Had enough, sir?' he said tersely.

Light and Shadow

The man jumped then regained composure. 'Quite enough, thank you.'

'Good. 'Cos it's the police next time, sir. If you get my drift?'

The older man flushed an angry red and left the building without answering.

The security guard popped into the little room set aside for the gallery's part-time lecturers and tour guides.

'I've seen that tall, beefy one off the premises, Miss. Don't think he'll be back.'

Megan Johnson looked up. 'Oh thanks, Jack.' She looked relieved.

'If it's any consolation,' said Jack. 'It's not just you. Dr Cook's been having trouble too.'

'What? Sebastian?'

Jack nodded.

'Sebastian stalked by a woman?'

'By a man, an older man.' Jack said.

'Good Lord! Well, I wonder if he'd be interested.'

'What? Dr Cook interested in the older man?"

'Oh no! I didn't mean that! Someone I know is setting up a service called '*Stalkback*'. The idea is to make the stalker feel stalked.'

'That sounds good! How much does he charge, this friend of yours?'

'She charges £250.'

'Nothing illegal or dangerous involved, I hope?'

Light and Shadow

'Just a bit of information gathering, I think,' said Megan. Then added, 'Would you keep a check on the tour groups for me for a while, like you do?' she asked. 'I'd feel safer?'

'Of course. It's my job!'

Megan got up and gathered her things together to leave. As she got to the doorway, she rose up on tip toe and planted a chaste kiss on Jack's cheek.

'Thanks!' she said.

Jack smiled at the young woman affectionately. Daft they were, these arty boffin types. But you couldn't help liking them.

Our 'educated, romantic and discerning gentleman' was back home in Kent. Placing a mug of creamy coffee on a coaster, he sat down, looking dubiously at his laptop. Weird stuff had been going on with it lately. He'd received a strange message a couple of days ago and clicked on something, he wasn't sure what. But it seemed, after that, somebody might have taken over his laptop. The cursor moved around all by itself in an unnerving manner and a strange screen came into view.

Delaying for a minute, he crossed the lounge and drew back the curtains. Misty, murky weather outside. He walked back to the table and opened the lid of his laptop. He was hoping for his usual slew of messages from the dating sites. Normally he got a good haul, ensuring an enjoyable morning of messaging. The screen woke up okay but then the cursor started moving around on its own again. Then the screen changed. It was as if he was looking at someone else's screen. Damn. It was happening again. Capital letters started to appear, white against a black background. Jumping about. Zooming in and out, pixellating, forming words, threatening words. A logo flashed up that said *Stalkback*. He closed the lid of his laptop, smartly.

He stared into space, shocked. In his mind's eye, he could still see the white words. The threats. Yesterday, the messages had said

Light and Shadow

that they knew where he lived. They knew his phone number. The phone had rung. Just three times and then stopped. Now, suddenly it rang again, four times. And then stopped. He walked to the wall and pulled the landline out of its socket. Alarmed, he walked to the window and stared out, scanning the misty street for strangers. Just then there was a knock at the door. He waited a minute. Another knock. He went to open the door.

'Morning, William. I hope you're well?'

With initial relief, William saw it was only Isobel, his dowdy, irritating neighbour who, obviously smitten with him, kept popping round and inviting him to things. Blasted woman.

'I'm fine thank you. Trust you are too?' William said with forced civility.

'Weather's not very nice,' said Isobel. 'But it's supposed to brighten up later?'

William waited. He noted her tight, low-cut top revealing an unpleasant area of skin the texture of crumpled tissue paper. Huge smears of eye shadow and roughly applied bright red lipstick. Trying way too hard, he thought, wondering, not for the first time, how old she was.

'Haven't seen you about lately? Been gallivanting?'

He said nothing. Waited, distracted.

'Er, well, the thing is,' Isobel said looking at him cheerily. 'I *was* going to a concert this afternoon with a friend but, unfortunately, he's not well and can't come. So, I've got a spare ticket. I wondered if you might like to come. It's at the old theatre. A tribute band is playing music from our sort of era. There's even dancing! Could be fun?'

God Almighty, thought William, appalled. It took him a few seconds to think of a reply.

'In fact, I shall be going up to town shortly for a date with an opera singer,' he lied. 'So, I can't help you out I'm afraid.

Light and Shadow

You can no doubt get your money back if you can't persuade anybody to go with you,' he added coldly.

Isobel chuckled. 'Chasing one of your young ladies in London again, eh? Never mind. I'll ask Leonard from Number 32. He'll be glad to get out.' She turned to go. 'Bye!' she said with a merry wave, 'Have a great date with your, er, opera singer!'

William stood in his doorway for a moment, muttering, '*Our era* indeed! The cheek. When's she going to get the message and leave me alone? Bloody stalker.'

The Valley of the Shadow

After the divorce, the law courts settled that the two children, Paul and Philippa, should go to visit their father on his farm in Wales every school holiday. Their mother, not liking the idea one bit, wrote to someone near the farm that she knew slightly asking him to visit and check up on the children when they were there.

'I've asked Ed to visit you on the farm,' she said to them.

'Who's Ed?' Paul asked.

'You remember. He's that nice man I met when I lived down there. He writes a fishing column for the local paper. English. Quite educated. I'll ask him to pop in regularly. That way he can tell me if anything odd happens. So, don't be surprised when he turns up.'

So, when they were down there and he did turn up, they weren't. Except for the noise. They were used to the sound of the neighbour's dog barking through the clear air from the hill opposite. They knew the fast patter of the water pump, pulling gallons of fresh water from the stream up to the water tank behind the house. The gentle suck suck of the milking machines in the cow shed was familiar to them too. As was the clatter and hum of the generator that ran the machines. They could hear the difference between the Fordson and Ferguson tractors as they droned and sputtered, ploughing and harrowing in the higher fields. Most especially though, there was the sudden deep silence in their valley when the generator was switched off in the evening, after milking. Then came the throaty caw of rooks, filling the quiet air with fullness, as the birds settled in the treetops at dusk.

Light and Shadow

They knew, like an old friend, the sound of the nine o'clock plane to Ireland. Their father would watch as it flew overhead, winking lights in the night sky, punctuating the end of his working day.

But when they heard the throb of a massive motor bike coming down the lane one afternoon, all of them, Grandma, Grandpa, Dad, Paul and Philippa, stopped what they were doing and listened. The bike got louder and louder and eventually roared into the yard, all shiny chrome and bright red metal. The man in leathers astride it, swerved expertly to avoid the cow pats, then manoeuvred as close to the concrete pathway as he could get. He planted his legs wide, switched off the noisy engine, swung off, set the heavy bike on its stand, and took off his helmet.

Philippa had never seen him before. She glanced at her brother. Paul didn't seem to recognise the man either. Their Dad did though, and walked over to him in his slow, calm way. The two men chatted for a bit before they all trooped in for tea.

Philippa didn't take much notice of the conversation. Just ate a little of the bread, butter and jam and one of Grandma's welsh cakes.

But as the stranger stood up to leave after tea, he suddenly addressed her,

'Well then, would you like to ride up to the top gate on the motor bike, Pip? You can open it for me if you like.' He said it like it was a huge treat.

A worldly-wise adult these days would probably have known right then, right there. But the little girl seemed to be the only one surprised. 'How did he know my nick name is Pip?' she thought. 'How did he know I like opening gates for Dad? Why did he think I was interested in motor bikes, when I'm not? Why did he ask me?' She was the baby of the family at six years old. She stared at him. He spoke again.

Light and Shadow

'You could open the top gate for me. Then she can run back, can't she?' he said to her Dad. 'I won't go too fast,' he added reassuringly.

'That's all right,' said Dad. 'You can go if you want to, Pip?'

She didn't know if she wanted to or not, but it seemed to be settled anyhow. Outside again, the man climbed onto the front of the bike. Dad lifted Pip onto the back and they showed her where to rest her feet. She was told to put her arms round Ed's middle.

'Hang on tight!'

Ed revved the throttle with his right hand a couple of times and they bumped slowly out of the yard, him using his legs now and then to balance. Then he pulled his legs up, placed his feet on the rests and they started the climb up the lane, taking the double bend quite fast and streaming on for the next half mile.

It was cold, windy and uncomfortable so, having tried out this new sensation, Pip was glad to clamber off at the top gate and open it for him. She closed the gate after him in her favourite way, giving it a push and then jumping onto the bottom bar for the swinging arc back, holding on tight for the crash against the gatepost.

He'd parked his motor bike at a tilt again. He was the other side of the gate.

'Did you enjoy that then?'

'It was okay.'

'Climb up on the gate. I can't hear you,' he said, taking off his helmet.

She climbed up until she was standing on the third bar. Her face was level with his. It looked very close.

Light and Shadow

'Well, I'll be off now. I'll see you again soon. Give us a goodbye kiss then.'

Instinct stirred in her and she did not move.

'Come on. Just a peck on the cheek.' He turned his face and pointed to where. She hesitated then leaned forward obediently and made herself touch her mouth lightly to the side of his face. She wheeled away then, suddenly repulsed, jumped down off the gate as fast as she could, and tore off back down the lane to the farmhouse.

Her Dad was waiting for her in the yard.

'Did you like the motorbike, love?'

'No,' she said and picked up some stones to throw for the dog.

Ed popped in a few more times while they were down there that summer, usually on a Sunday afternoon about teatime. Sometimes he arrived in an old van packed full of fishing gear, rods, lines, boxes of lures, nets, a stool, ground proof sheets. The father didn't go fishing himself but he listened over tea to the talk about different local streams. The idea came up somehow that one afternoon Ed would take the two children a little further up their own stream to a spot with a deep pool. He would show them how to fish there. Neither Paul nor Philippa said they wanted to go but, somehow, it was all settled.

So, one Sunday, Ed, carrying a load of gear, and with the two kids trailing slowly behind him, tramped upstream. The spot they arrived at was very overgrown. Willow trees hung over the dark water pool, trailing tendrils of silvery leaves into the surface of the water. Thick bushes lined the stream banks and, in the clearing by the brambly path, the grass grew lush and thick.

Light and Shadow

'OK, we'll put the gear here,' said Ed in the clearing. 'And check we've got everything.' He started laying out equipment on the grass. Paul and Philippa wandered a little further off, as if to play.

'Did you want to come fishing?' Paul whispered.

'No. Did you?'

'No. I don't like him.'

Ed called them over.

'Now look, Paul,' he said to the boy. 'I've gone and left the middle part of this rod on the front seat of the van. You'll have to run back and get it.'

'I'll go with him,' said Pip quickly.

'No, there's no need,' said Ed. 'You'll just slow him down. He can run faster on his own.'

Paul looked at his sister. She looked back at him. Some sort of understanding went between them.

'Be quick!' she whispered, not wanting to be alone with this man.

'I will,' said Paul and he ran off fast down the path. Ed watched him go. Then he laid out a ground sheet and sat down on it cross-legged. Feeling his eyes on her, Pip wandered away and tried to play, vaguely skipping and jumping in the grass.

'Come over here' said the man that her Mother had asked her to trust.

'I'm all right here,' she said.

Light and Shadow

'It's nicer over here,' he said.

She came just a little closer.

'Come and sit down.'

'I'm all right here.'

'Come here and sit down with me a second.'

By the time Paul came hurtling back, out of breath, panting up the path, with a short section of fishing rod in his hand, Pip was standing far off in the clearing. Ed was assembling bits of equipment.

Pip didn't know if it rained then. Or whether they fished. She couldn't remember how they got home.

He didn't come back that summer.

Back at school, in Somerset, in the autumn, in a scripture lesson one afternoon, they were studying passages from the bible. The first bit somehow stuck in Pip's mind,

'Follow me! Follow me and I will make you fishers of men.'

She started thinking about fishermen. Fishers of men and fishers of little girls.

Then the class looked together at a psalm. As they read it through, the words on the page began to jump about and she suddenly started to feel dizzy. Old words and new words rang in her head.

Light and Shadow

'My Mother made him my shepherd. (I did not want.)

He maketh me to lie down in green pastures.

He leadeth me beside the still waters.

I was in the presence of mine enemy.

His fishing rod and his staff did not comfort me.'

She was sick all over her desk and then she fainted. When she came to, she was in the school sick bay. She was there for a while and then they let her go home early.

Years later, Pip was down in Wales visiting her Dad, now happily remarried, retired, but ill. They were walking, very slowly, round his local reservoir. It was a cloudy day and the water looked dark.

'Do you remember that Ed bloke, that fisherman?' he asked. 'The one your Mother insisted keep an eye on you?'

'Yes, I remember him distinctly.'

'Did I ever tell you? He was found in a shed, sleeping with a boy. The man who found him was, I think, the boy's own father. And he shot him. The father of the boy shot Ed with a gun. He killed him.'

She could see the scene in her mind's eye, as if she was right there. She could see, close up, in detail and colour, a shed overgrown with ivy, cracks in its yellowed plaster walls, a black metal door latch, the thin mattress on the floor. She saw the father coming in. The boy pinned down. The father's rage. She heard the shots from the father's gun. And saw Ed dead. And the boy, terrified but freed from him.

Light and Shadow

'Good!' she said. The loudness of her own voice surprised her. 'Good! I'm glad!' she said loudly again, exultant.

They kept on walking slowly, father and daughter, arm in arm, along the path around the reservoir, in silence. Words went round in her head, again and again.

'I was in the presence of mine enemy.

Now he is dead and my cup runneth over. Ed is dead and my cup runneth over. Ed is dead.'

(This story was first performed at the Power of Women Festival 2022)

Shacks (A one-sided dialogue)

The Gallery Attendant stands up. He approaches courteously. But she says,

... Oh, don't worry, I wasn't going to touch it! No. I just wanted to see what it was made of. Looks like little pieces of wood and cardboard glued together. And then this one has little pearly buttons all around the door for decoration.

... Yes, I do. I really like it. See, I thought from the poster outside it was just going to be paintings. I didn't know it was going to be these little house sculptures, all shapes and sizes and bright colours. And the white shelves set them off so nicely!

... Was there? No, I didn't see it. I haven't seen any other exhibitions. To tell you the truth, this is the first time I've been in here. 'Course I walk past the building every morning on my way to work. But I've never thought of coming in.

... Why not? Well, for one thing I didn't know it was free. And then I thought it'd be full of, well, you know, arty types! That's why I waited til mid-week and came early. To avoid the crowds.

... Oh, you go ahead. Take the weight off your feet. I bet you get tired standing around in here all day. Me? I clean at the newspaper offices in Saul Street. Round the corner.

Light and Shadow

... Well, no not really. I can't say they *are* good employers. I mean they're alright if you just stick to cleaning. But the other day I went to the, what do you call it...Human Resources Department? Bloke in there says, 'Clean in here later, please!' I told him I hadn't come to clean his office. Said, I want to know how I can get an office job here. He looks dead surprised. Asks me what qualifications I have. So, I tell him I had to leave school early to look after Mum. She had sickle cell, you see. Died when I was fourteen. Yes, it was, terrible. Years ago now, of course. Anyway, I said all about how I was learning computing at the library and wanted to make a change. Better pay, you see and you get holidays, sick pay, that sort of thing, with an office job. Well, he wasn't interested. Just told me he didn't think he could help. Well, you know what they're like. So much for Human Resources. Should say, 'Inhuman Resources' on the door!

... What made me come in today? It was the poster that did it. Every time I walked past the front of the building, I saw that picture of the little shack. Not a great big dolls house like you sometimes see on TV. But a makeshift little place, made from bits and pieces. All cheerful, colourful and warm. It reminded me of home somehow.

... No, we never lived in a shanty like that. We were in a council flat. Very plain. But we kept it nice. Sky blue curtains and Dad painted the front door bright red. I used to love the sight of that red door coming home! The picture of the little house on the poster made me feel that way too. Plus, the woman who made these little structures, Beverly something?

... Oh, thank you! Can I keep this? Yes, I see now, Beverly Buchanan. Yes, well, my daughter's name is Beverly too. Spelled the same way. So that made me curious too.

Light and Shadow

... No, my daughter's not an artist. She's working in a care home at the minute. Anyway, I wanted to see if the little wooden house pictured on the poster was a copy of a real house. And if it was, who might have lived there. ... Oh, I see! It says, 'Modelled after self-built rural residences lived in by African Americans in the South where the artist grew up.' Fancy that. And I'm guessing that, just like these little toy houses here are put together with bits of old cardboard and stuff, in real life they'd have been made of all sorts too. Cos the people would have been poor, wouldn't they? And just trying to make a shelter out of anything they could find. Out of nothing, probably.

... My favourite little house? Well, there's one in the other room. A small shack made of green boards, sitting on red stilts, and standing on a bit of plywood. It's got a sloping roof, pale blue. And there's a big orange chimney up the side. It's roughly made but decorated with bottle caps. No windows. Tiny door. The shingles have got cracks between them. If it was real, you couldn't possibly live in it. It looks so ramshackle. But it's personal somehow. Friendly. Humble. I felt so happy looking at it, I almost cried.

... Another three weeks yet til the exhibition closes? Oh, I'll come again then. Now I know it's free.

... You mean this visitors' book here? I see lots of people have written in it already. Well, alright, but I won't put my name in. What could I put? I could write about how clever she is to make things that are so simple and yet so beautiful. Who'd think that humble little shacks, the size of bird houses, made out of odds and ends, by a woman in America, could end up in a famous art gallery in England! Makes you think, doesn't it? Maybe the meek really *can* inherit the earth.

Light and Shadow

… No, you go on. They look like kids on a school visit. You'll have your hands full with them!

The Gallery Attendant nods and moves gently towards the school group.

(This story was first broadcast on BBC Radio Kent Upload on September 21st, 2022)

Light and Shadow

Angels in the Air

Ruby had never really thought about angels before. Not even realised that most of this musical piece was about them. She'd been handed her hire copy of the score, by the choir librarian, some weeks before they'd started to use it in rehearsals. She'd noted the composer, Benjamin Britten, and then popped it in her bag to take home.

The next weekend, having a few minutes before 'The Voice' came on the telly, she'd opened up her copy of 'The Company of Heaven' and found, to her dismay, that the person who'd had the hire copy before her had been a copious scribbler. Ruby sighed, sat down at the kitchen table, and set to, vigorously rubbing out the pencil marks. The blasted previous user of the score had not only marked the start of each soprano line with a smudgy, graphite arrow, but had covered each page with warnings to herself in capitals, like 'BREATHE EARLY!!!!!' and 'STAY QUIET HERE!!!!!!!' It took Ruby ages to get rid of all the pencil marks, the graphite murmurings, the exclamations of the past soprano ghost.

The hired copy now feeling more her own, Ruby took it to rehearsals for the next two months. The Britten piece was hard to rehearse. The choir just came in here and there, in unexpected places, pitches and harmonies. Ruby was so busy trying to keep up that she never really noticed what the piece was about. And as she couldn't sight read, played no musical instrument, and was the only person in her entire family to be the slightest bit interested in choral music, rehearsals had been difficult.

Now, on the night of the concert, she sat on the staging in the cathedral. Dressed in black, like 200 others, she gripped her folder and, at the conductor's dignified signal to rise, she stood up slowly to face the audience.

People would, she thought, probably assume that the body of singers standing before them were all music teachers, or talented

Light and Shadow

instrumentalists, professionals even. Ruby, being none of these, felt a fraud. But she pushed the feeling down. Now was not the time for selfish emotions. It was the time for watching the conductor, assuming the stance of a real singer and singing.

Except that, although they had been stood up, they were not actually singing in the first part. The conductor stood with his back to the audience, facing the orchestra and the choir, and waited, not just for people to stop coughing and whispering, but for actual pin-dropping silence. He got it. His baton came down and the piece began.

Ruby looked down from her place in the eighth row, over the heads of singers below her, down to the stone floor of the cathedral where the orchestra was seated. She often thought that, being a singer on the staging, she got the best view in the house. From there, she could see the violinists leaning, sweeping, swaying, as they bowed. She could see the necks of the woodwind players puffing out and pinking with effort. The man with the triangle counting, hitting his silvery instrument precisely, and then gently killing its sound with his fingertips on the metal. The soloists rose from their wooden chairs on the podium to face the audience. Ruby could only see their backs, the bass and tenor in evening jackets, the soprano and alto chilly in their backless, evening gowns. She spotted the narrator, standing up in the pulpit, doing knee bends to un-cramp his tense legs.

Now that Ruby had the chance to listen to the whole Britten piece being performed, she found it much more inventive and imaginative than she'd expected. The section called 'The Creation' featured a Big Bang. In the part called 'War in Heaven', the men in the choir roared a wonderfully aggressive chorus, and in another sublime section, the first and second sopranos entwined their voices delightfully. The altos got most of their entrances and timings right. Ruby got her breathing nervously wrong in one bit, but she didn't disgrace herself.

Light and Shadow

But she'd certainly never really thought about angels before tonight. There they were, on the cover of the concert programme, pictured in tender, yellow-gold. They were mentioned by name in the text inside too. Michael the Archangel, the Cherubim and Seraphim, Raphael, Gabriel, and the rebel angel Lucifer, were all named in the cast list.

Ruby listened as the narrator in the pulpit told the audience the story of angels, the first beings that God made, creatures pure as light. As he spoke on, her imagination came alive with the idea of angels many-winged, with golden pinions, leaving their bowers, praying, singing, playing silvery lyres. Little glittering spirits, with the wind whistling through their golden wings. Gazing past the massive stone columns of the nave, through the air to the stained-glass windows above the West door, Ruby thought she could *almost* see them, their soft feathers contrasting with the hard stone. She could *almost* hear their wings rustling, see their bright feet, their little bare toes, as they flew and flitted. She *almost* saw their golden hair flying, their heads ringed with fiery halos. The story, the music, the singing, the air, the vaulted stone ceiling, the stained-glass windows, all fed her imagination.

The piece came to an end. The conductor, his arms still uplifted, held them all waiting, in a trance, as the sounds of the orchestra and the choir gradually cleared from the ringing stones of the cathedral. Everyone held their breath, spell bound. Even the angels looked about them. Then, the conductor slowly lowered his arms. The choir relaxed. The clapping of the audience began.

As the choir sat down, Ruby turned to her neighbour. 'I've never really thought about angels before,' she remarked. 'Do you suppose they're related to fairies?'

'I'm not really into spirits of any kind,' replied the neighbour, dryly.

Light and Shadow

And, on hearing that, the wing-ed ones, whether related to fairies or not, hovered in the air for a moment, disappointed, and then, with feathery fluttering, they were gone.

(This story was first broadcast on BBC Radio Kent Upload on March 25 and 26, 2021)

Light and Shadow